The Enchanted Woods

The Five Mile Press

Once upon a time, a little girl called Sarah Jane lived in a pretty cottage at the edge of a wood. The trees in the wood grew close together and on hot days she liked to sit in the shade and play with her toys.

There were ferns and flowers growing thickly between the trees and patches of wild strawberry plants. One warm sunny day, Sarah Jane wandered into the woods to play with her toys and look for wild strawberries.

Leaving her toys beneath a tree, she wandered further into the forest and found a few strawberries to put in her basket. All the while she had the strangest feeling she was being watched.

Eventually, she came to a big old tree and under the tree was a ring of mushrooms.

It was a magic fairy ring. But Sarah Jane didn't see it until after she had stepped inside. She stared at it, puzzled, and wondered what it was.

Suddenly Sarah Jane glimpsed a
procession of fairies winding through the
trees. Some were quaint and impish, and
others were the most beautiful creatures
she had ever seen.

"Sarah Jane," they cried, "you are
needed in Fairyland. Now that we've
caught you in our magic fairy ring we
can take you with us."

Then they waved their magic wands,
and Sarah Jane felt herself become
smaller and smaller.

She was now no taller than the fairies, and felt as light as thistledown. The fairies took her gently by the hands, and together they flew up above the treetops and out over a shimmering sea.

They landed on the shores of a strange and beautiful land. The flowers were taller than they were, and huge butterflies waited to greet them.

Soon, a messenger arrived from the fairy palace.

"Sarah Jane," he announced, "the Fairy King and Queen have been told of your arrival, and they would like to see you now."

So the fairies sat
Sarah Jane on
the back of a
butterfly, and
together they
flew over a lake
to the fairy
palace, whose
golden turrets
sparkled in the
morning
sunlight.

The King and Queen
welcomed Sarah Jane, and
told her why she was needed
in Fairyland.

"Our daughter is to be
married to a prince from a
neighboring kingdom," said
the Queen. "We need the
presence of a mortal to ensure
their good fortune and a happy
marriage."

"Yes," said the King. "You will
bring them good luck. Come,
you will be our honored guest
and join us in our celebration."

Soon, it was time for the wedding.
The chatter and laughter of the guests
grew quiet as they gathered to watch
the Prince and Princess exchange wedding vows.

After the wedding, a magnificent banquet was held in the glittering hall overlooking the lake. Sweet music was played by a band of funny little musicians while everyone, including Sarah Jane, feasted on the finest delicacies Fairyland could offer.

When the banquet was over, it was time for the Prince and Princess to leave. Together, they descended the golden stairway, as their guests cheered and showered them with rose petals. Then they climbed into a golden carriage drawn by dragonflies and flew off to their new home over the hills.

Now it was time for Sarah Jane to return home too. The fairies flew with her over the sea, and back to the fairy ring in the woods. They waved their magic wands, and once again she became her normal size.

"Goodbye, Sarah Jane," they said, dropping feather-light kisses upon her cheek. "You will always be our special friend."

Then she found herself alone in the woods once more with her basket and her toys beneath the shady tree.

Sarah Jane looked at her basket in amazement. It was overflowing with small, delicious strawberries. She picked up the basket, and her toys, and wandered home. Her family found it hard to believe her wonderful tale of how she had been a guest at a fairy wedding. But certainly, no one had ever seen so many wild strawberries as she had in her basket. They agreed that it must be a gift to her from the fairies, a sign to show she really *had* been to Fairyland.